Zack Giallongo

BROXO

NEW YORK & LONDON

First Second
NEW YORK & LONDON

Published by First Second
First Second is an imprint of Roaring Brook Press,
a division of Holtzbrinck Publishing Holdings Limited Partnership
175 Fifth Avenue, New York, New York 10010

Distributed in the United Kingdom by Macmillan Children's Books,
a division of Pan Macmillan.

Colors by Braden Lamb with Carly Monardo

Cartography by Matthew Loux
Broxo's Lullaby by Alexander Danner
Font created by John Green
Book design by Rob Steen

Cataloging-in-Publication Data is on file at the Library of Congress

ISBN: 978-1-59643-551-3

First Second books are available for special promotions and premiums.
For details, contact: Director of Special Markets, Holtzbrinck Publishers.

First edition 2012

Printed in China by Macmillan Production (Asia) Ltd., Kwun Tong,
Kowloon, Hong Kong (supplier code 10)

10 9 8 7 6 5 4 3 2 1

For Dad.

BEAST TEETH MOUNTAINS
PERYTON LAKE
ULITH'S KEEP
PERYTON VILLAGE
GLOTH'S LAIR
FELLMOSS CAVES
FROGTEAR SPRING
HUR HUR TREE
ACK STAG
OREST
VARLI'S GARDEN
NETHERGULCH
TO OUTLAND SLOPE
ZIRCO NESTS
GROVE OF THE OLSHEC
GRAMMA'S HIDEOUT (BROXO'S HOME)
THE DEAD GRONT
MUDPITS
GOAT GRAVEYARD
HOFARA'S CLEAVE
DEAD PINE BROTHERS
ZORA CLIMBS HERE
HANGBATS LIVE HERE
PERYTON PEAK

CHAPTER 1

AND SO I´VE CLIMBED PERYTON PEAK...

...FOR NOTHING.

AT LEAST I'LL BE DRY IF IT RAINS IN THIS AWFUL PLACE.
WHICH IT PROBABLY WILL.

GOODNIGHT, FLAME.
DON'T DIE ON ME.

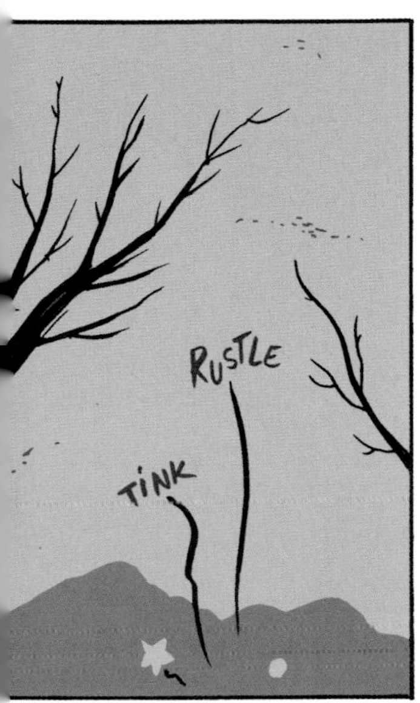
RUSTLE
TINK

HEY!

GET OUT OF MY STUFF!
AH!
DON'T TOUCH ME!

FLING!
BOOT!

SHINK!

HER GIANT FOOT STRUCK ME!
SHE THREW ME IN THE MUD! CHECK MY FUR FOR DIRT! JUST CHECK FOR ME!

WE MUST HAVE REVENGE ON THIS OUTLANDER!
GLOTH WILL KILL HER!
OR WE CAN TELL THE MASTER.

IS YOUR MASTER OF THE PERYTON CLAN? I DEMAND YOU TAKE ME TO HIM!
DEMAND?!

FAT CHANCE, O TREE-LEGGED ONE!
YOU'D DO BEST TO LEAVE THIS PLACE.

I AM THE PRINCESS OF-
LOOK!
HAH?

HA
HA
HA

PRINCESS OF IDIOCY, MAYBE!
SHE'LL BE WALKING WITH THE DEAD SOON ENOUGH!

SIGH

I'M GOING TO STARVE IF I DON'T HUNT.

I DON'T *WANT* TO HUNT!

SHHNN

WAH!
CHop!

ZUZU! I´M SORRY! I ALMOST TOOK OFF YOUR-

HEY, WAIT!

BOY! WAIT!
I NEED YOUR HELP!

PLEASE DON'T RUN!

AH!

BOY?

ROARR!

huff
huff
huff

SLAM!
AAAAAAAH!!!

WHAM!

SNRT

PANT!
PANT!

pant
pant

SLUMP

DAD, PLEASE COME GET ME!

CHAPTER 2

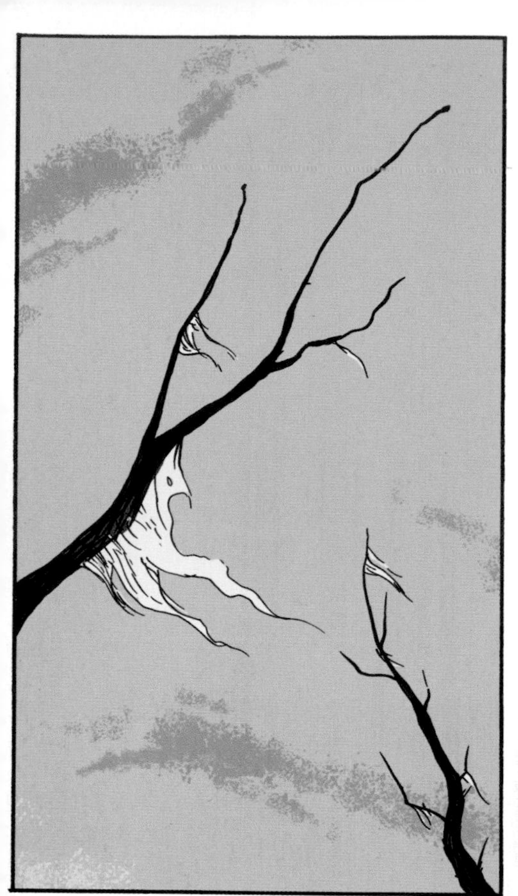

WATER!

SNIFF
SNIFF

OH...!

UM, EXCUSE ME?

HELLO?

CRK!

MUR!
SHRIEK!

SWACK!

AARR!

WAUGH!

BONK!

ARE YOU A DEMON?
WHAT?

Sniff
Sniff

UH, THANKS FOR SAVING ME. I-

SHAKE
SHAKE
HUH?

DEMONS HATE WELB ROOTS!

RIGHT, WELL... I'M NOT A DEMON.
I'M ZORA OF TETHEDE, PRINCESS OF THE GRANITEWING CLAN!

I AM BROXO, KING OF ALL-MOUNTAIN!

AND THIS IS MIGO. HE IS SORRY HE SCARED YOU BEFORE.
SNRT

IF YOU *WERE* A DEMON, YOU WOULD BE SAFER.
CREEPERS ARE *BAD TROUBLE*. YOU SHOULD GO.

UH, H-HEY! WAIT!

I'M COLD AND LOST AND REALLY, REALLY HUNGRY!

PLUS, I LOST MY GEAR WHEN YOUR *THING* CHASED ME!
SO YOU KINDA OWE ME.

TOSS!

HOME NOT FAR. YOU HOP UP!
NO WAY!
BUT ZORA WALKS SLOW.

TOO BAD!

THERE YOU ARE!

MOTHER WAS GETTING WORRIED!
PAT
PAT

SOMEONE IS HERE, MASTER.
OH?
AND SHE THREW US IN THE MUD LIKE TRASH!

POOR KOL AND KROL! VANITY IS SUCH A BURDEN!
SHE'S AN OUTLANDER LOOKING FOR THE PERYTON CLAN.

BROXO FOUND HER.
WHAT IF SHE DISCOVERS YOU AND TELLS THE PENTHOS?

SILENCE!

MASTER, PLEASE!
YOU EELS!
WE JUST WANT YOU TO BE SAFE!

WHOOOOOSH!

KRA-KOOM!

YOU'RE RIGHT. I'M SORRY.

THERE IS MUCH TO CONSIDER.

BUT FOR NOW, I NEED REST.

HOY!
OVER HERE!

SHE SAID SHE WAS BANISHED! WHY WOULD A CLAN BANISH A CHILD IF THEY DIDN'T HAVE GOOD REASON?
BECAUSE THEY'RE BARBARIANS!

IF WE TURN HER OUT, SHE'S DEAD.
EVEN A SMALL LEAK CAN RESULT IN A FLOOD.

WHAT SAY YOU, ORTHO?
I BROUGHT THE GIRL HERE. IF SHE'S ALLOWED TO STAY, I'LL CARE FOR HER.

AND WHAT OF THE LAKE AND THE STAG?
QUIET! ALL OF YOU!

I NEEDN'T REMIND YOU THAT IN THE WAKE OF MY HUSBAND'S DEATH, WE STILL HAVE A KING.

SPEAK, ARROX.
WELL...

IF I WAS TRAPPED IN THE SNOW AND RESCUED, I WOULDN'T WANT TO BE KICKED OUT AGAIN.

THEN IT'S SETTLED.
SHE STAYS, AT LEAST THROUGH THE WINTER. I WILL CONSULT THE ANCESTORS ON THIS. AND FOR NOW, SHE WILL NOT TAKE PART IN THE LAKE CEREMONIES. AGREED?
AYE.
TOK!

ULITH! YOU MAY ENTER.

CHAPTER 3

SO, YOU'RE PRETTY YOUNG TO BE KING, EH?
IS YOUR CLAN BIG? MINE IS. BIGGEST IN THE PENTHOS. I THINK...

ALSO, WHY IS IT SO DESOLATE HERE?

I HOPE THERE'LL BE GOOD FOOD WHEREVER WE'RE GOING. I'M STARVING!

AND I MEAN, I *AM* A VISITING PRINCESS!
SO I ASSUME THERE'LL BE SOME FORM OF BANQUET AND BATHS AND-

ZORA MUST LEARN TO *KEEP QUIET* OR SHE WILL WAKE THE CREEPERS!

BLEAGH!
PTOO!

COME ON, ZORA!

UH... I DON'T THINK YOU GET IT. I NEED TO GO TO YOUR *VILLAGE*. LIKE, WITH YOUR *PEOPLE?*

YOU... DON'T LIKE IT?
OH, BERK.

IS THERE NO VILLAGE HERE? PLEASE TELL ME YOU'RE THE VILLAGE IDIOT AND YOUR CLAN THREW YOU OUT!
WHAT?

THE PERYTON CLAN LIVES UP HERE! WHERE ARE THEY?

CAN YOU TAKE ME TO THEM?
DO NOT KNOW.

I HAVE TO SET MY LIGHTS.
COME ON, MIGO.

LIGHTS KEEP BAD TROUBLE AWAY. ZORA SHOULD COME.

THANK YOU, LITTLE LIGHTS.

ZORA! TIME FOR EATS!
FINALLY!

COZY.
WE CAN COOK HISSERS ON THIS!

CHOMP

HPTHOO!

SOMETIMES THE HEADS DO NOT COME OFF ALL THE WAY WHEN I CRUSH THEM.
BERK!

SO...
YOU'RE UP HERE
ALONE?

NO.
THERE IS
MIGO.
AND
ULITH.

WHO IS
ULITH?
SHE IS A
WITCH!

SHE IS NOT
BAD, BUT SHE IS
STRANGE.
GLOTH,
THOUGH. HE IS BAD.
BUT A COWARD.
I SEE.

SO...
WHAT ABOUT THAT
THING EARLIER TODAY?
YOU SURE CHOPPED
THAT UP GOOD!

ER...
DONE.

OOPS! YOURS IS TOO DONE!
GREAT.

SO...
IT'S KIND OF A BIG DEAL THAT I'M HERE, DON'T YOU THINK?

I CAME ALL THE WAY FROM TETHEDE IN THE EAST. HOME OF THE GRANITEWING CLAN. NOT THAT YOU ASKED.

DO YOU EVEN KNOW ABOUT THE FIVE CLANS OF THE PENTHOS?
UH HUH.
REALLY?
NO.

RIGHT. LOOK.
THIS IS THE PENTHOS. THERE ARE FIVE CLANS.
MINE IS HERE, EAST OF THE UNMAR RIVER.
SCRRR
YOURS IS *WAY WEST*. AT LEAST, I THOUGHT IT WAS.

EVERYBODY STAYS IN THEIR OWN LANDS NOW. BUT MY FATHER'S TRYING TO GET EVERYONE TOGETHER. WE GRANITEWINGS ARE ALREADY TRADING A BIT WITH THE DHALEDANS AND THE NORDS.

I CAME HERE TO TRY TO MEET THE PERYTONS. BUT THERE'S NO ONE HERE!
I AM HERE! AND MIGO!

YES, THAT'S FANTASTIC, BUT WHERE ARE YOUR PEOPLE? YOUR MOTHER AND FATHER?
GRAMMA LIVED HERE, BUT SHE LEFT A LONG TIME AGO.

GREAT.
WHERE ARE YOU GOING?
OUTSIDE.

STAY IN THE LIGHTS! AND DO NOT PEE BY THE ROUND ROCK. THAT IS BROXO'S PEE SPOT!

MAYBE I GOT THE WRONG PEAK?
I MIGHT'VE MESSED UP.
ARE THE PERYTONS ALL DEAD?
THIS IS A DISASTER!
I COULD STEAL SOME FOOD AND GO HOME...

EXCEPT I DON'T KNOW WHICH WAY TO GO!

SNRT!
WAH!

WHAT IS WITH THESE THINGS?

THERE'S NO WAY HE CARVED THEM.
HMPH
DON'T QUIT, ZORA.

FIND OUT WHAT HAPPENED HERE AND WHAT THAT WALKING CORPSE WAS ALL ABOUT.
SOMEHOW.

DID YOU PEE?

IS THAT ANY OF YOUR CONCERN?

SO, UH...
WHERE SHOULD I SLEEP?

HERE?

I DON'T THINK YOU'RE PICKING UP WHAT I'M PUTTING DOWN, BOY.
THE PROPER THING WOULD BE FOR YOU GUYS TO SLEEP OUTSIDE WITH THE OTHER FILTHY ANIMALS AND LET ME SLEEP IN HERE!
BUT THIS IS BROXO'S HOME AND I SAID YOU COULD STAY!

OKAY, OKAY. TURN YOUR HEAD.
WHAT? WHY?

BECAUSE I'M DISROBING, IDIOT!

SHE THINKS I NEVER SAW A BUTT BEFORE?

IT WILL BE COLD OVER THERE...
HMPH

CHAPTER 4

BZZ...
HEY...

BROXO?

BROXO?

HEY, WHERE'S BROXO?
ZZZZzz

HEY!
"FLICK"

I CAN'T BELIEVE I JUST DID THAT...
SNORT
ZZZZzz

BROXOOO!

A LAKE?

drag
drag

SO MUCH FOR
BATHING.

HELLOOOOOOOO!

TRIP!
WAH!
CLINK!

WHAT THE-?
HE SAID NO ONE ELSE LIVED UP HERE.

THIS STUPID THING MUST'VE BEEN HERE *FOREVER!*

SPLOOSH!
UNF!

BROXO!
IF YOU'RE STILL ON THIS DAMN MOUNTAIN...
I'M LEAVING!

SO LONG, PERYTON BOY!

AH!

HE-HELLO.
DO YOU KNOW WHERE
BROXO IS?

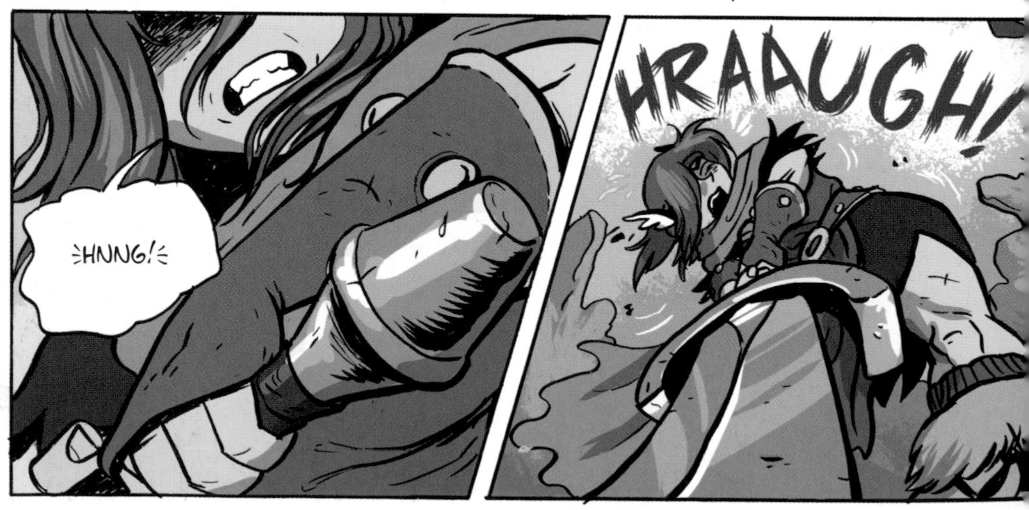
HNNG!
HRAAUGH!

KA-
THUNK

SPLASH!

SPLSH!
SPLSH!

CRACK!

ZORA!!!

IT GOT MY SWORD!

CLIMB!

AAAHHH!

HURK
PLEASE DON'T LET GO!

APUGH!
SHLSH!

RUN!

WAIT!
BROXO!

IT REALLY BURNS!
TRY!

ZORA MUST RUN!
CHOK!
BOOT!
WHUMP!
SHUNK

SWIPE!

THEY CANNOT DIE, ZORA!

BOOM!

SHAKOOOOM!

CRACKLE

HURRY.

THEY WON´T STAY DOWN FOREVER.

THEIR SCRATCHES ARE NASTY.
UNTREATED, YOUR LEG WOULD TURN GREEN, THEN YOU'D GET SICK, AND ONCE THE VOMITING STARTED, THERE'D BE LITTLE HOPE LEFT.

BUT I THINK YOU'LL BE FINE.
SWIPE!

THE BEES MAKE STRONG HONEY HERE. IT WILL DRAW ALL OF THE NASTINESS OUT.

THANK YOU, ULITH.
NOW YOU WON'T THROW UP TO DEATH.
Pat

ULITH, MAY I ASK YOU SOME QUESTIONS?

DO YOU KNOW ABOUT THE PERYTON CLAN? ARE YOU PART OF THEM? BECAUSE YOU LOOK LIKE A-
KLAK!

HEH.

WHEN KOL AND KROL TOLD ME ABOUT YOU, I KNEW WE'D CROSS PATHS AND HAVE THIS CONVERSATION.

OBVIOUSLY, I'M NO PERYTON.

BUT ZORA...

YOU ARE A STRANGER IN MY LANDS AND A GUEST IN MY HOME. YET YOU QUESTION *ME*?
HOW RUDE.

UH-OH.
I JUST...

AND AFTER I SAVED YOUR MISERABLE LIFE!

YOU MIGHT BE A PRINCESS IN YOUR LAND, BUT YOU'RE NOTHING IN MINE.

NOW, LET'S SEE. PAYMENT...
TAP
TAP

PAYMENT?
IT'S LIKE A TRADE.
I KNOW THAT, DUMMY.

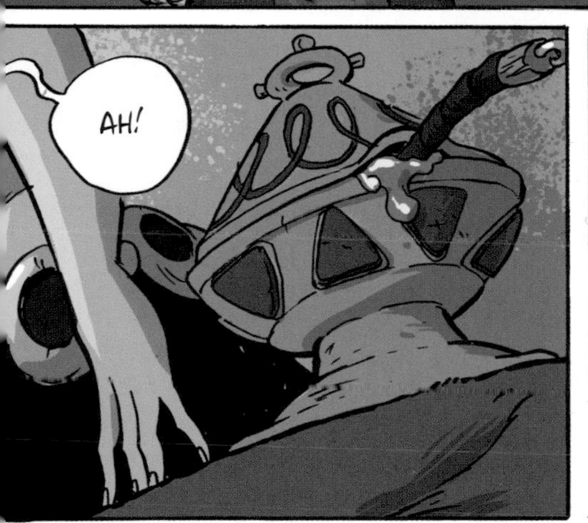
AH!

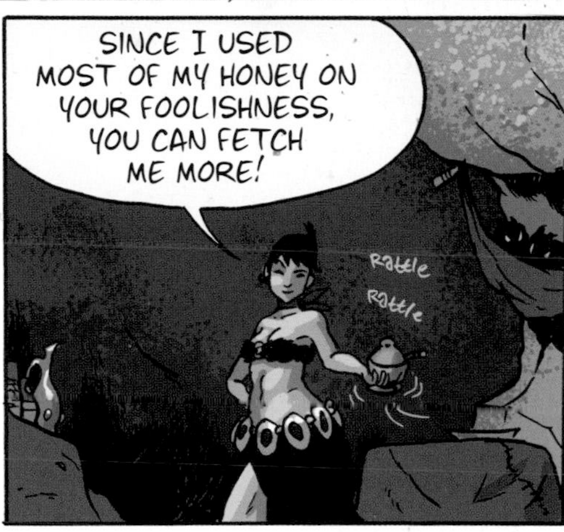
SINCE I USED MOST OF MY HONEY ON YOUR FOOLISHNESS, YOU CAN FETCH ME MORE!
Rattle
Rattle

UH... BUT... GLOTH HAS BEEN HUNTING IN THE GROVE LATELY.

OH COME NOW, BROXO! SURELY YOU'RE NOT AFRAID, ARE YOU?
BESIDES, GLOTH ONLY HUNTS AT DAWN.

ANYWAYS, HONEY IN RETURN FOR RESCUING YOU IS HARDLY AN ADEQUATE WAY TO REPAY ME, BUT IT'S A START.
EWUP

WELL THEN, GREAT AND WISE ULITH, PLEASE ALLOW US TO HUMBLY VACATE YOUR PRESENCE BEFORE WE INCUR ANY MORE DEBT!
THANK YOU FOR YOUR KIN SERVICE!

OH, AND ZORA?

NEXT TIME I SEE YOU, WE'LL DISCUSS PAYMENT FOR THROWING MY BABIES IN THE MUD.
STAY DRY!

THERE'S A WORD FOR PEOPLE LIKE HER.
REALLY?

HEY, ZORA. WAS THE SWORD YOU LOST THE ONE FROM MY WALL?
UH, YEAH. I'M SORRY!
OH. IT WAS MY GRAMMA'S SWORD.
GROAN

CHAPTER 5

UH HUH

I WENT THERE A LONG TIME AGO.

SPLASH!

BROXO!

THIS IS NOT A GAME! COME OUT!

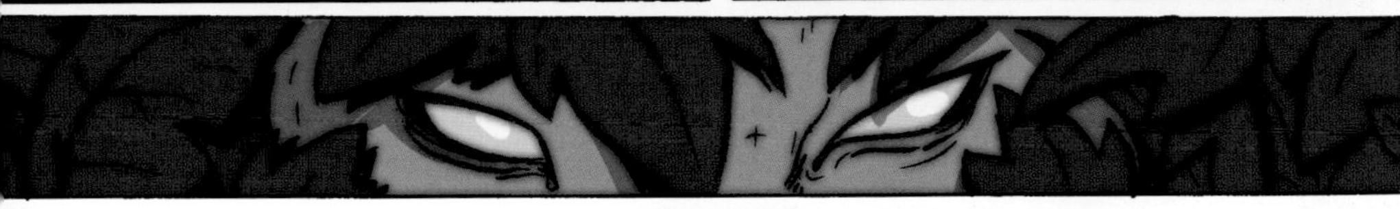

IF YOU DON'T COME OUT NOW, I'LL FIND YOU AND SKIN YOU LIKE SO MANY SKEEKS!
GASP!

RAAR!

BRAT! I SHOULD-

BROXO!
FREEZE!

SHNNN!

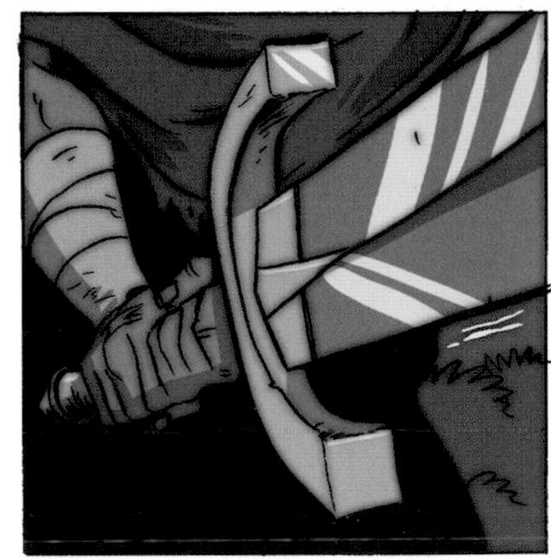

AAH!

ROLL ROLL

UNF!

GRAMMA!

GRAMMA!!!
SHUNK

HUFF
HUFF
GRAMMAAAA!!!

A BLACK STAG? LIKE THE ONE ON YOUR BLANKETS?
IT WAS RIGHT BEHIND HER, BUT GRAMMA SAID SHE NEVER SAW IT.
SHE LEFT AFTER THAT.

LEFT?
I DUNNO.

GASP

...BEAUTIFUL!

HUZ HUZ STINGS DON'T HURT MIGO!
SNIFF SNIFF

SPLURTCH!
LAP LAP LAP

SO HE DOES THE WORK.
BUT HOW DO YOU-

ULITH DOESN'T KNOW ABOUT THIS PART!
GROSS!
SPLOOOOK!

HMMMMZZZZZZZ

BZZ!

THE MOUNTAIN IS SO BLEAK...
YOU'D NEVER EXPECT A PLACE LIKE THIS.

WE CAN STAY FOR A LITTLE.

EEK!
HA!

OH!
LOOK!

OH... FINALLY, SOMETHING THAT'S NOT MEAT!

WANT SOME SKEEK?
NO-
WAIT!

SHOW ME YOUR ARM!
HEY!

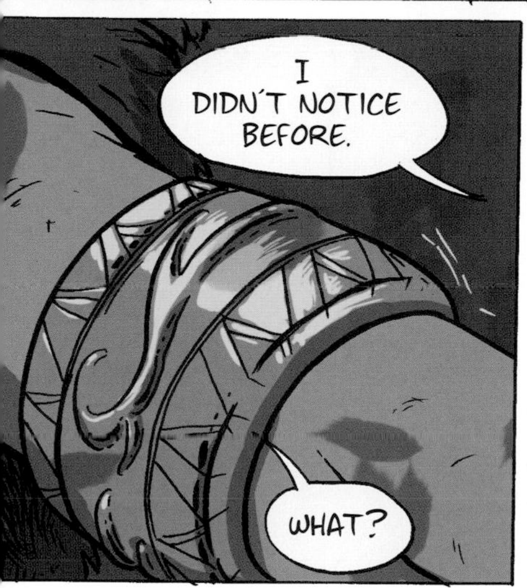
I DIDN'T NOTICE BEFORE.
WHAT?

NOTHING...
YOU MADE BROXO DROP LUNCH FOR "NOTHING"?

NEXT TIME, BROXO WILL KNOCK LUNCH FROM YOUR HAND FOR "NOTHING"...!
OH, WHINE WHINE!

YOU SOUND LESS LIKE A KING AND MORE LIKE AN OLD...

...LADY.

ZORA! COME QUICK!
AH! WHAT NOW?

IT'S MIGO!

GO LOOK!

HE MADE THE BIGGEST POOP I. HAVE. EVER. SEEN!

MUDSNAKE! YOU HAD ME SCARED!

SORRY! WE SHOULD GO SOON.
RUB RUB

HMPH
BROXO? DO YOU LIKE IT HERE?
OH! LOOK!

NOT IF IT'S POOP!
NOPE!

NOT EVEN A LITTLE.

KKS!
POOR THING!
KKSSS!
KSS!

THE PIT IS ONE OF GLOTH'S TRAPS. HE'S A COWARD.
DON'T *YOU* USE TRAPS TO HUNT?

I DON'T HAVE HUGE TEETH AND CLAWS.
TRUE.

GLOTH WILL COME FOR IT SOON. AND THEN WE WILL HAVE ***BAD TROUBLE***.
WAIT! YOU'RE GOIN TO LEAVE IT

WHAT IF *YOU* WERE IN A TRAP?

OKAY, OKAY.

BROXO WILL DO IT.

KSSSSSS!
SSSSS

COME ON, MUCK FACE.
TAP TAP

HE LIKES YOU.

FSHT!

ARGH!

AHH!
OH!
OH, BERK!
IT STINKS!!!

AHH!
HELP!
NO WAY!
YOU STINK
WORSE THAN
BEFORE!

I CAN'T OPEN
MY EYES! IT SMELLS
SO BAD!

HUGS ARE THE
ONLY CURE!
AIR OUT,
STENCH BOY!
FLING!

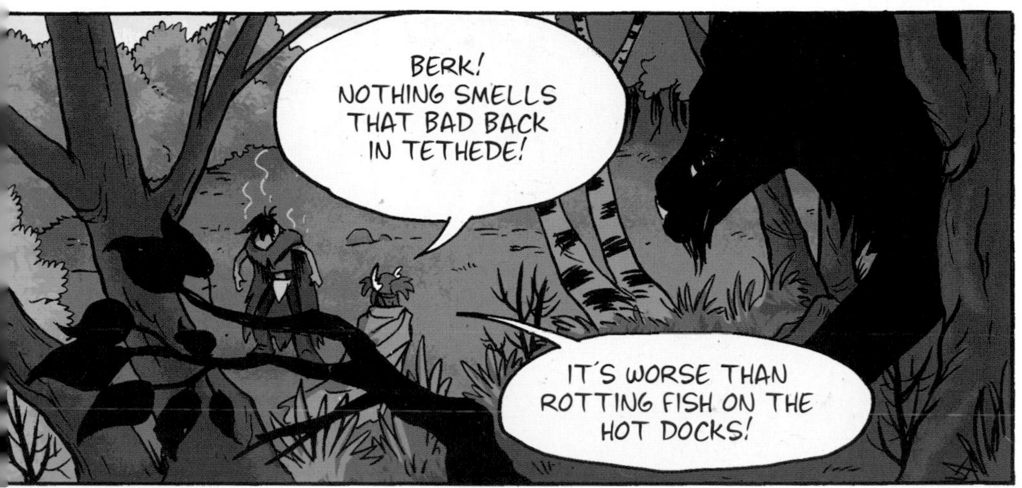
BERK!
NOTHING SMELLS THAT BAD BACK IN TETHEDE!
IT'S WORSE THAN ROTTING FISH ON THE HOT DOCKS!

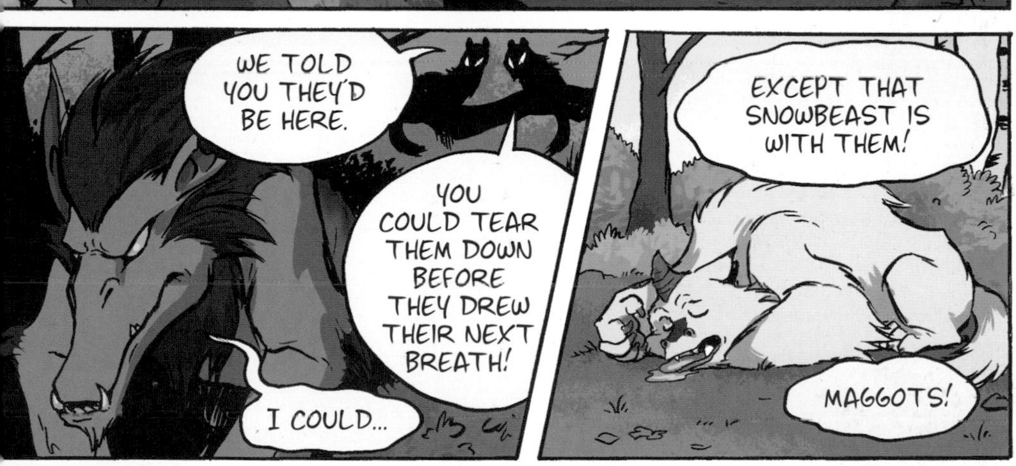
WE TOLD YOU THEY'D BE HERE.
YOU COULD TEAR THEM DOWN BEFORE THEY DREW THEIR NEXT BREATH!
I COULD...
EXCEPT THAT SNOWBEAST IS WITH THEM!
MAGGOTS!

TO BE FAIR, HE *IS* SLEEPING.
SO CRAWL DOWN THERE AND CHEW HIS EARS AND EYES OUT. OTHERWISE, DON'T WASTE MY TIME!

CLEARLY WE MISREAD THIS HUNTER'S HEART. YOU'D THINK HE'D WANT TO AVENGE HIS MOTHER!
CLEARLY.

SNARL!
YOU MAGGOTS AREN'T WORTHY TO BE MY MEAL.
HISSSS!

OR MY SUBJECTS WHEN I'M THE ONLY KING ON THIS MOUN-
SNIFF
THAT WIND...

ANCESTORS! UP HERE?
THOSE SCREECHING WELPS MUST HAVE ATTRACTED THEM.

TELL YOUR WITCH THAT BROXO'S BLOOD IS OWED TO ME AND I PLAN ON COLLECTING.

NO ARGUING IT, NATURE BOY...

Sniff
Sniff
NOW YOU REALLY NEED A BATH.
POK!

I'LL GET THE HONEY POTS SO WE CAN GO.
HOW CAN SOMETHING SO SMALL SMELL SO BAD?

HEY, BROXO! WHAT'S OVER THAT RIDGE?
HUH?

I SAY
WHAT'S-

OH NO!

THUNK
BROXO!
CREEPERS!
BUFF!

RUN,
MIGO!
THE HONEY
POTS!

SMASH!

CHAPTER 6

SIGH

I CAN'T TELL IF THE WATER IS ACTUALLY NICE OR IF I'M TOO TIRED TO CARE.

WOOOOO!
SPLASH-
KING!

BROXO?!

KER-
SPLOOSH!

I TOLD YOU TO STAY ON YOUR SIDE!
IT'S TOO ROCKY THERE.

AND STOP STARING!
I'MBB NBBOT!

WHERE ARE YOU GOING?
SPLISH

HEY! CAREFUL OVER THERE!
SPLISH
I'D REALLY LIKE SOME PRIVACY...!

PRIVACY? IS THAT A KIND OF FISH?
NO! IT'S- URR...!

UNF!

HEH... TANGLED...
BLUSH!
SPLSH

THANKS.
WAIT.

UH...

TWIG.

SO WHAT ARE YOU GOING TO DO ABOUT THE HONEY?

DUNNO. NEVER SAW CREEPERS THERE BEFORE.
BLEAH!

MAYBE WE CAN JUST FORGET IT.
YEAH.
WE DON'T OWE THAT WITCH ANYTHING.

PLUS HER HEAD LOOKS LIKE A VEGETABLE.
AND WHY DID SHE ACT STRANGE WHEN I ASKE
ABOUT THE PERYTON CLAN?

SHLUP!
I THINK SOMETHING REAL FOUL HAPPENED UP HERE THAT SHE KNOWS ABOUT. I THINK THE CREEPERS *ARE* THE PERYTONS!

STOP.

OKAY. SORRY.

MAYBE SHE'S NOT THE ONLY ONE WITH SECRETS.

IF THERE ARE NO PERYTONS, WILL ZORA LEAVE?

DO YOU WANT ME TO?

NO.

MY FAMILY MUST BE SO WORRIED.
FAMILY?

MY FATHER, BROTHER, AND SISTER. MY MOTHER DIED A YEAR AGO.
IT'S BEEN HARD.

MY BROTHER AND SISTER ARE A LOT OLDER THAN ME. THEY'VE WORKED HARD ON MY PARENTS' DREAM OF REUNITING THE FIVE CLANS.
BUT THEY DON'T CARE ABOUT ME AT ALL.

SNIFF
SO I LEFT WITHOUT TELLING ANYONE. I WAS HOPING THEY'D THINK I DIED, YOU KNOW?

AND THEN I'D RETURN MIRACULOUSLY WITH THE PERYTON CLAN BEHIND ME!
BUT OBVIOUSLY THAT'S NOT GOING TO HAPPEN.

I GUESS I NEVER THOUGHT IT'D BE SO HARD TO MISS MY FAMILY.

I WAS STUPID TO COME ALONE.

NOT STUPID. ZORA IS SMART.

BUT SINCE THERE ARE NO PERYTONS, WHAT WILL YOU DO NOW?

THERE ARE OTHER CLANS TO FIND.

I THOUGHT MAYBE...

YOU'D COME WITH ME.

I...
DON'T KNOW.

BUT THERE'S NOTHING HERE! AND YOU'D NEVER SEE ULITH OR THE CREEPERS AGAIN!

THIS IS HOME.
I LIKE IT HERE.
REALLY? IS IT THE TURD-COLORED SKY? THE CONSTANT, INESCAPABLE DANGER?

THERE'S NO DANGER IF YOU'RE CARE-

ZORA! FREEZE!
WHAT?

SKREEE!
AAHH!
SHOK!

GYAH!
WHUMP!

SHOVE
WAUGH!

MAYBE WE GO BACK NOW.
GOOD THOUGHT.
MUNCH
MUNCH

HELP!

HELP!

HELP US!

HE CHOSE YOU.
CHOSE YOU TO SAVE US!

TO FREE US!
FREE US!

NO!
FREE US!

BRAT!
WELP!
HE'S NOT OUR CHILD!

SPLOOSH!

BROXO!

COME ON!

NOOOOOO!

WHAT HAPPENED?
NOTHING!

I´M FINE. GOING TO FIND FOOD. I´M FINE.

COME, MIGO!

I'M TIRED OF HISSERS. LET'S GO TO THE GROVE AND GET SOME BIG FOOD.
Pat Pat

SWW!

THOK!

THIS BOW IS A PIECE OF JUNK. WISH I HAD MINE BACK.
HOYYY!

FINALLY! GONE LONG ENOUGH?
COME SEE WHAT WE GOT!

CLOPTOES ARE HARD TO CATCH, BUT KING BROXO AND MIGO DID IT!

DRAG
DRAG

A HORSE!
THERE ARE *HORSES* UP HERE?! YOU DON'T EAT HORSES!

IF YOUR BACK FACES THE SKY, YOU CAN BE EATEN.

BEAST!

IDIOT BEAST!

I WAS STARTING TO LIKE YOU!
BUT YOU'RE JUST A DUMB ANIMAL!

BROXO KNEW EVERYTHING BEFORE ZORA CAME!
ZORA RUINE
EVERYTHING

ZORA RUINED EVERYTHING!

CRUNCH

STARVE!
FINE!

RUN AWAY LIKE A SCARED ANIMAL!

YOU THINK I NEED YOU? I DON'T NEED A STUPID ANIMAL!

I HATE YOU!

CHAPTER 7

HE'S BEEN GONE A LONG TIME.

I'M GLAD YOU STAYED, MIGO.

IT WOULDN'T BE NICE TO BE ALONE.

LOOK AT THESE KNOTS!

I BET I CAN GET RID OF A FEW OF THESE BEFORE DARK.
PURRR

HELP US...!
I CAN'T!

STAG SAVE US!
WHERE IS THE BOY?!
HELP!
SHHH...
NO TIME FOR TEARS, LITTLE KING.
LISTEN.

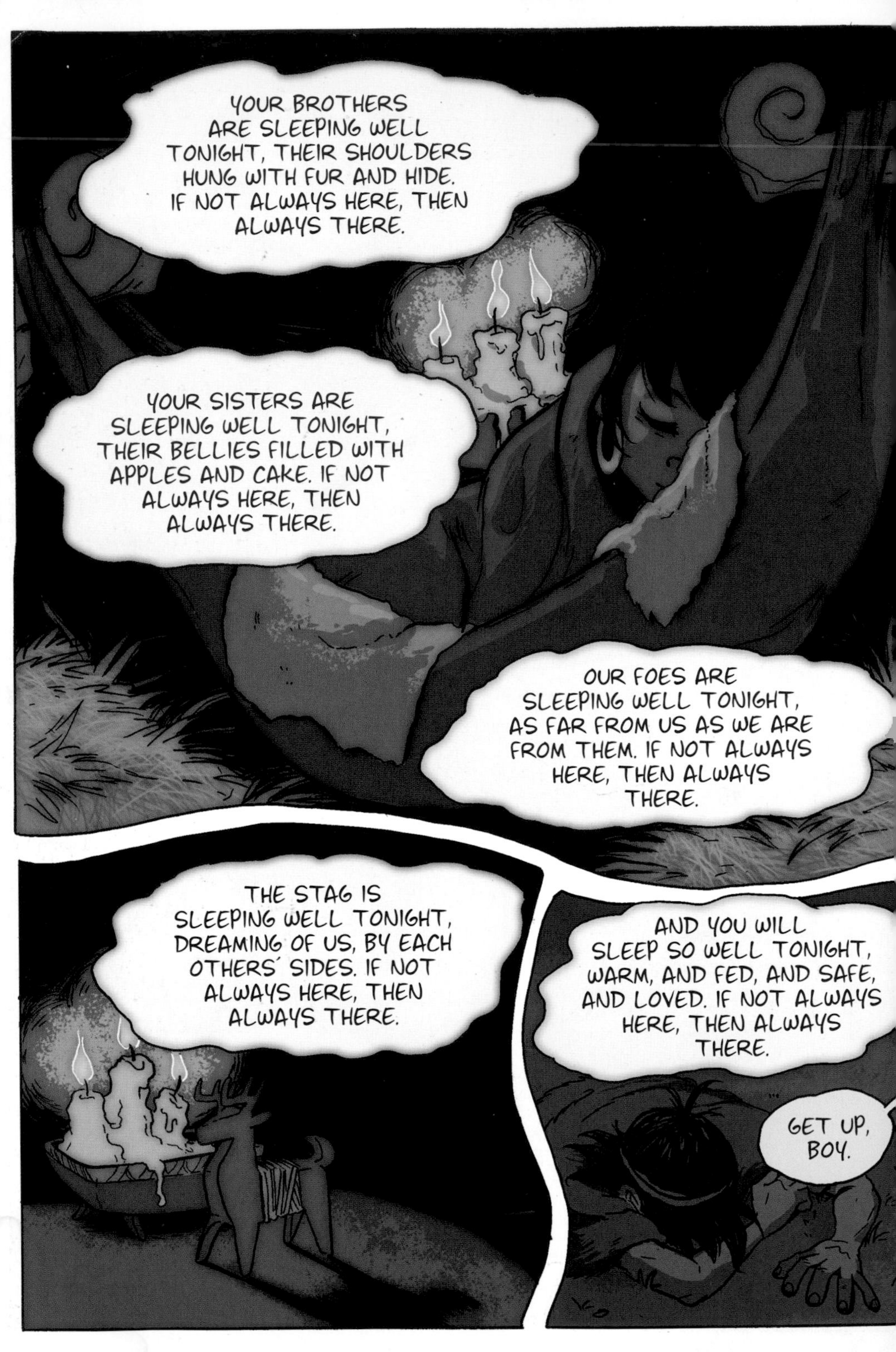
YOUR BROTHERS ARE SLEEPING WELL TONIGHT, THEIR SHOULDERS HUNG WITH FUR AND HIDE. IF NOT ALWAYS HERE, THEN ALWAYS THERE.
YOUR SISTERS ARE SLEEPING WELL TONIGHT, THEIR BELLIES FILLED WITH APPLES AND CAKE. IF NOT ALWAYS HERE, THEN ALWAYS THERE.
OUR FOES ARE SLEEPING WELL TONIGHT, AS FAR FROM US AS WE ARE FROM THEM. IF NOT ALWAYS HERE, THEN ALWAYS THERE.
THE STAG IS SLEEPING WELL TONIGHT, DREAMING OF US, BY EACH OTHERS´ SIDES. IF NOT ALWAYS HERE, THEN ALWAYS THERE.
AND YOU WILL SLEEP SO WELL TONIGHT, WARM, AND FED, AND SAFE, AND LOVED. IF NOT ALWAYS HERE, THEN ALWAYS THERE.
GET UP, BOY.

WHO'S THERE?
SO BIG NOW!

SKINNIER THAN YOUR FATHER, THOUGH.
ULITH?

ULITH? HOW DO YOU KNOW HER? YOU'RE NOT CAROUSING WITH HER, ARE YOU?
SHNK
SHOW YOURSELF!

YOU BRAT, HOW DARE YOU?

PULLING A SWORD ON YOUR POOR DEAD GRANDMOTHER!
IF I HAD A BODY, I'D KNOCK YOURS CLEAR ACROSS THE PENTHOS FOR THAT!
G-GRAMMA...?

FMP

IT TOOK ME SO LONG TO GET BACK. HOW LONG HAS IT BEEN?

YOU'RE SKIN AND BONES! DOESN'T MIGO KEEP YOU FED?
AND WHAT'S THIS ABOUT ULITH?

DOES SHE STILL EXIST? YOU'VE MET HER, I TAKE IT? AND WHY ARE YOU STILL HERE ON THE PEAK?
GRAMMA!
EH?

WHY DID YOU LEAVE ME?!

NO...

NO, BOY.
NEVER.

BUT I REMEMBER. YOU LEFT AND SAID YOU'D RETURN. BUT YOU DIDN'T! NOT EVER!
I'M SORRY, BOY.

YOU DIDN'T DESERVE ANY OF THIS.

BE STRONG FOR GRAMMA, NOW. WE HAVE WORK TO DO.
WORK?

AH, BOY. YOU'VE FORGOTTEN MUCH. BUT MUCH YOU NEVER KNEW.
LISTEN TO GRAMMA...

DO YOU REMEMBER THE STORY OF PERYVALN?
YES.
REALLY?
NO.

PERYVALN WAS THE *OM* OF OUR CLAN, AN IMMORTAL THAT LED OUR PEOPLE AFTER THE PENTHOS WAS MADE.
BEFORE HE LEFT, HE TAUGHT US THAT HIS GREAT STAG, THE PERYTON, WOULD WATCH OVER US...

EVERY HUNDRED YEARS, THE STAG WOULD LEAD OUR SPIRITS TO THE UNDERWORLD.

FOR SEASONS IMMEASURABLE, WE GAVE THE BODIES OF OUR DEAD TO THE LAKE AND SUMMONED THE STAG WITH THE WYLERN.

IT IS VERY SPECIAL TO SEE HIM. MOST OF US WILL ONLY EVER SEE HIM IN DEATH.

BUT BROXO- CAN YOU REMEMBER THE NIGHT OUR PEOPLE DIED?

I'M... NOT SURE...

ARROX, MY SON AND YOUR FATHER, WENT MISSING.
THE SKIES CHURNED.

AND WE WEREN'T READY...

FOR OUR ANCESTORS TO ATTACK.
KRAK-OOM!

MOTHER!
GET TO GALIA!

THE BODIES WE'D GIVEN TO THE LAKE WERE ALIVE!
OUR LOVED ONES HAD RETURNED AND BROUGHT HELL.

BUT WE COULD NOT DEFEND AGAINST BOTH THE FURY OF OUR ANCESTORS AND THE TERRIBLE STORM!

GALIA! COME WITH ME NOW!
THE BABY!
WAH AH HUNH! WAH!
KKRRRRK
RUN, OLD WOMAN!
I LOVE YOU, BROX-!

MIGO! WHERE ARE YOU?!
TAKE THE BABY AND RUN!
WWRR
HELL WOULD HAVE BEEN A PEACEFUL EXPERIENCE.

WE LOOKED FOR OTHER SURVIVORS, BUT THE ANCESTORS STILL MADE GOING TO THE VILLAGE TOO DANGEROUS.
YOU HAD TERRORS EVERY NIGHT.

I COULD NEVER SORT TOGETHER WHAT HAD HAPPENED.
IF NOT FOR YOU, I MIGHT'VE LOST MYSELF.

FINALLY, I DECIDED WE WOULD LEAVE PERYTON PEAK AND THROW OURSELVES UPON THE MERCY OF ANOTHER PENTHOS CLAN.

ALONE, I WENT TO THE LAKE TO PAY MY RESPECTS.
ARROX...?
I WAS FILLED WITH GRIEF ALL OVER AGAIN WHEN I FOUND YOUR FATHER'S REMAINS...

...AND MORE CONFUSION.
YOU!

THE NORD GIRL HAD RUN AWAY FROM US YEARS AGO.
WHAT ARE *YOU* DOING HERE?

ME?! MOTHER OF MUCK, WHAT ABOUT YOU?
HOW ARE YOU STILL ALIVE AND DEFILING THIS SACRED PLACE?

WE HAD TAKEN ULITH IN AS A CHILD. BUT SHE WAS DIFFICULT, STRANGE, NOT ONE OF US.
SHE LATER FLED WHEN ARROX CHOSE YOUR MOTHER.

YOU PERYTONS WERE ALWAYS SO SECRETIVE ABOUT YOUR WAYS! AND NOW THAT NO ONE'S LEFT, YOUR SECRETS ARE TRULY DEAD!
YOU BELIEVE I HAVE NO RIGHT TO BE HERE.
AT LEAST ARROX *TRIED* TO APOLOGIZE, EVEN AFTER CHOOSING GALIA!

WHAT HAPPENED TO MY SON?

MAYBE THE PERYTON CLAN PAID FOR ITS FOOLISH TRADITIONS?

YOU UNGRATEFUL, LITTLE-! WE TOOK YOU IN! FED YOU! CLOTHED YOU!
MADE SURE I WAS NEVER ONE OF YOU!

RUMBLE
ONLY ARROX KNEW WHAT I WAS! KNEW MY POWER!
AND HE PAID THE PRICE!

YOU ALL PAID THE PRICE THAT NIGHT.

MURDERER!
DON'T!

CRACK!

SSSSSSSSS

plip

plip

plip

CHOOM!

POW!

pant
pant

ANOTHER ONE!

WHAT KEEPS DISTURBING THEM?
IS IT THE WING GIRL?

NO.
SOMETHING ELSE. I CAN FEEL A... SHIFT, MAYBE.

OUR DAYS HERE ARE NUMBERED.

CHAPTER 8

THIS IS GRAMMA.

ZUZU...!

NO GHOSTS IN YOUR CLAN, GIRL?
N-NOT REALLY...!

WELL, IT WAS AWFULLY BRAVE OF YOU TO JOURNEY SO FAR FROM YOUR HOME.
LUCKILY BROXO TRUSTS YOU. WE HAVE MUCH TO DO.
WE?

WHAT'S YOUR NAME, GIRL?
ZORA.
HOW POLITE.
ZORA...

I HEARD YOU LOST MY SWORD.
ERG!
BLUSH!

NO MATTER. YOU'LL MAKE IT UP TO ME.
OF COURSE.

IT'S NOT LIKE I HAVE MUCH USE FOR IT ANYHOW!
HA HA HA

SO, I UNDERSTAND ABOUT THE STAG AND ALL...

WHAT I WANT TO KNOW IS HOW *YOUR* SPIRIT IS FREE.
IT'S NOT EASY.

I KNEW I HAD TO GET A MESSAGE BACK HERE. I DIDN'T THINK IT WOULD TAKE TEN YEARS.

BUT I'M HERE NOW, AND WE MUST SUMMON THE STAG AT ONCE!
BUT THERE IS BAD TROUBLE. GLOTH LIVES NEAR THE RUINS.

SURELY MIGO CAN HANDLE A SINGLE SLAGCAT!
SNOR
UH-UH.

THE ONLY WAY THERE IS THROUGH A GAP IN THE RIDGE. MIGO'S TOO BIG TO FIT.
SKRTCH
SKRTCH
BECAUSE THE ANCESTORS ARE ALL OVER IT.
WE CAN'T GO THE REGULAR WAY...
BERK.

WELL, IT'S SIMPLE. I HEARD ULITH SAY THAT GLOTH THING HUNTS AT DAWN. ALL WE DO IS-
THERE'S NO "WE," GRANITEWING.

BROXO MUST RETRIEVE THE WYLERN ALONE. YOU'RE NOT PERYTON BLOOD. YOU WOULDN'T UNDERSTAND.

THERE *ARE* NO CLANS ON PERYTON PEAK ANYMORE.

HA! YOU'RE GUTSY, GIRL! THAT I'LL GIVE YOU! WHAT'S YOUR GREAT PLAN, THEN?

A TRICK FROM BACK HOME.
HOW DOES GLOTH FEEL ABOUT BEES?

COME ON! IF WE GET THERE BEFORE DAWN, WE'LL BE ALL CLEAR!
I'M COMING!

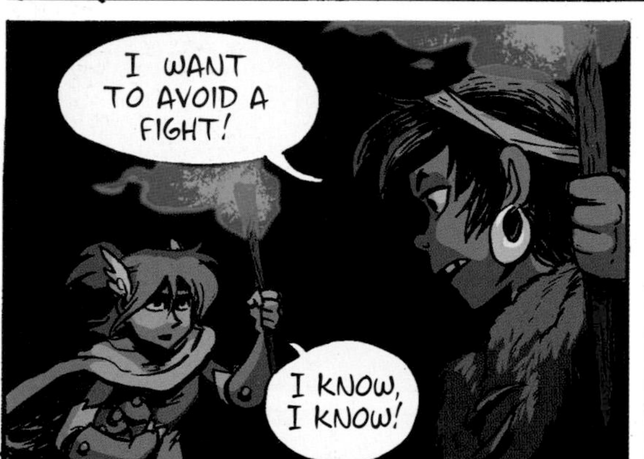
I WANT TO AVOID A FIGHT!
I KNOW, I KNOW!

CONSIDER MY TRIP TO THE GROVE AS A BIT OF "EXTRA ARMOR."

YOU SAID GLOTH'S A COWARD.
clink!
THAT DOESN'T MEAN HE'S NOT BAD TROUBLE!

WHIMPER
WE'LL BE ALL RIGHT.

BA-
BUMP
BA-
BUMP

STEP CAREFULLY.

SNAP!

WHAT HAVE WE HERE? IT´S BEEN A WHILE! TRESPASSING ON MY FRONT DOOR?

GLOTH! I THOUGHT YOU´D BE ASLEEP.
STREEEETCH!
NORMALLY, I WOULD BE.

BUT EVER SINCE THE STRANGER ARRIVED, MY SLEEP´S BEEN IRREGULAR.

NO TROUBLE THIS NIGHT. JUST LET US PASS.
TROUBLE? *ME?* I´M NOT THE ONE TRESPASSING!

SURELY WE CAN WORK SOMETHING OUT TO AVOID ANY TROUBLE.

STRANGERS ARE BAD FOR THE PEAK.
I COULD TAKE CARE OF HER.
STEP AWAY!

TELL ME WHERE YOU'RE GOING.
NONE OF YOUR BUSINESS.

NOT THAT OLD VILLAGE, I HOPE! IT'S DANGEROUS THERE!

EVEN I WON'T GO!
YOU'RE A COWARD.
AM I?

POUNCE!

WAH!

DASH!

THAT'S IT? HE'S GONE?!
GET IN THAT TREE!

WHAT? WHY? LET'S JUST GET OUT OF HERE!
NO!

I NEED ZORA TO GET MY BACK!

FACE ME, GLOTH!

RUSTLE

SWING!

HA HA HA
HOW DID YOU SURVIVE FOR SO LONG MAKING WILD ATTACKS AT THE DARK?!

I WORRIED THAT ULITH'S WALKING DEAD WOULD GET YOU BEFORE I COULD. BUT MOTHER WAS RIGHT - A PATIENT HUNTER GETS THE JUICIEST KILL!
ULITH'S WALKING DEAD? WHAT ARE YOU TALKING ABOUT?

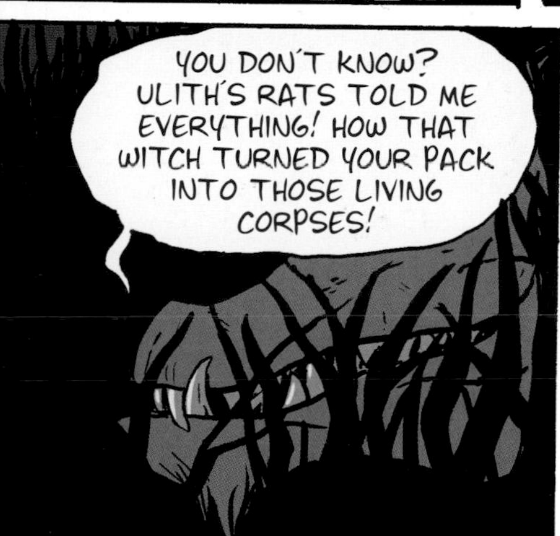
YOU DON'T KNOW? ULITH'S RATS TOLD ME EVERYTHING! HOW THAT WITCH TURNED YOUR PACK INTO THOSE LIVING CORPSES!

YOU'RE A LIAR!

IT BARELY MATTERS, NOW.
HEY. REMEMBER WHEN THAT OLD LEATHER WOMAN SAVED YOU AND KILLED MY MOTHER?

CHOOM!

SKID

AAH!
SLASH
STAB!
SKREEEE!
pant
pant
Hissss

PAF!

CHOP!

YOU DIE!!!

YAAH!!
SWIPE!
HA HA
HA
HA

EH?

THRASH
AROOooo!
THRASH

ADRA'S BONES!
HE'S STUCK!
MAGGOTS! YOU MAGGOTS!

I'LL HUNT YOU FOREVER!
THRASH!
WHEN I DESTROY YOU, THERE WON'T BE ENOUGH OF YOUR BODY IN MY DUNG TO COME BACK TO LIFE!

SHUT UP, SPIT-FOR-BRAINS!

FWOOOSH
PAF!
ROWR!

HURK!

YOU'RE ALL DEAD!

AAAARR!

AAAROOOO!

BYE, KITTY!

CAN YOU WALK?
HOW DID THE HUZ GET IN THE POT?

SMOKE PUTS THEM TO SLEEP.
WHERE DO YOU THINK YOU'RE GOING?
WOBBLE
WHERE DO *YOU* THINK?

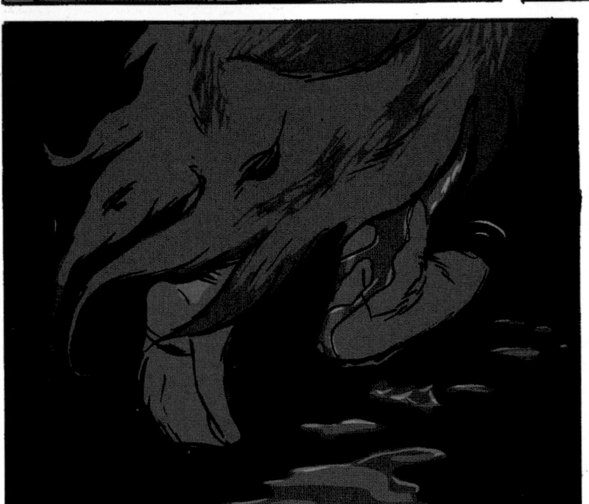

WE NEED TO GO BACK! YOU'RE BLEEDING REALLY BAD!

NO. WE'RE CLOSE.

CLOSE...
TO FIXING IT...

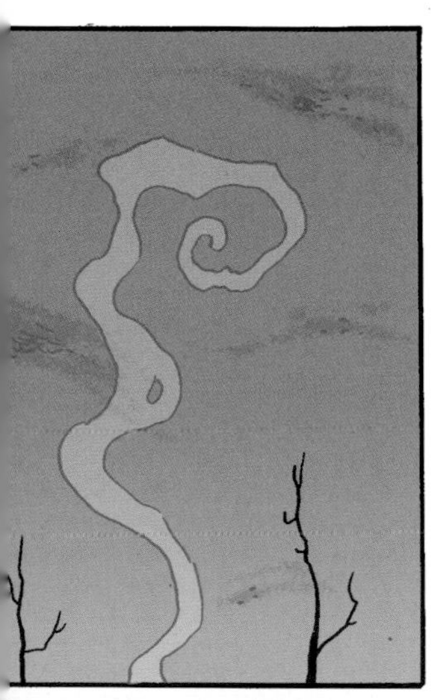

I FELT SOMETHING WRONG.
AS DID I. STILL DO.

YOUR KIND DON'T COME BACK FROM THE DEAD!
MMH.

I'VE FORGIVEN YOU FOR MY DEATH.
BUT MY SON IS A DIFFERENT MATTER.

ARE YOU HERE TO REPENT?

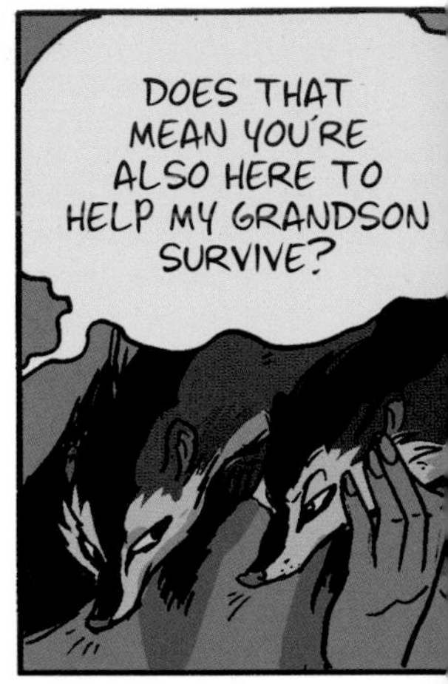

GRAMMA! BROXO'S HURT!

FAWNLING!
IT'S NOT SO BAD!
YOU!
WHINE
CARELESS AS USUAL!

GLOTH SLASHED HIM.
SHLUP

I FAILED, GRAMMA.

CHAPTER 9

HOY.
IS... IS THAT MY GEAR?

I FOUND IT BUT DIDN'T GIVE IT TO YOU BECAUSE I DIDN'T WANT YOU TO LEAVE.
BUT YOU NEED IT NOW.

HOW IS YOUR LEG?
fidget
ALL RIGHT. GLOTH DIDN'T GET TOO DEEP.

I WAS NOT CAREFUL. AND NOW THE PLAN IS MESSED UP.

BUT THEY ARE MY FAMILY. SO I'M GOING BACK FOR THE HORN.

WELL LUCKY FOR YOU, I'VE GOT A NEW PLAN.
I THINK IT'S OUR BEST CHANCE OF GETTING THAT HORN THING AND GETTING OUT OF HERE.

ALLOW ME TO ELUCIDATE, MY YOUNG APPRENTICE!
HUH?

IT RELIES ON A COUPLE OF THINGS. FIRST, IS THE HERD OF HORSES CLOSE BY?
SORTA.
SKTCH
ALSO, DO YOU THINK ULITH IS RELIABLE?

NO ONE TRUSTS HER. BUT I DO.

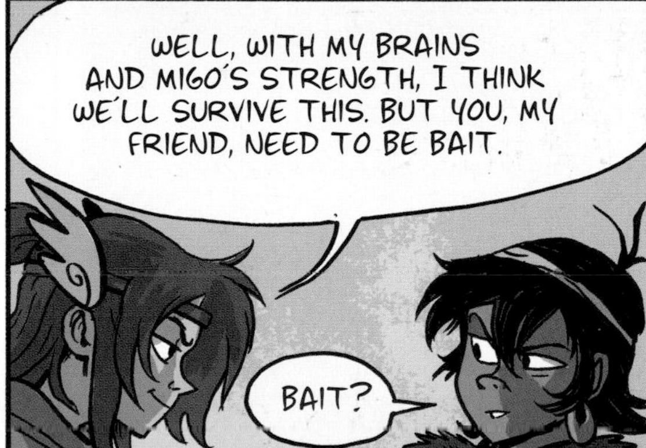
WELL, WITH MY BRAINS AND MIGO'S STRENGTH, I THINK WE'LL SURVIVE THIS. BUT YOU, MY FRIEND, NEED TO BE BAIT.
BAIT?

BUT I'M THE KING!

COME OUT INTO THE AIR I AM YOUR KING!

MURR!
MURR!

GULP

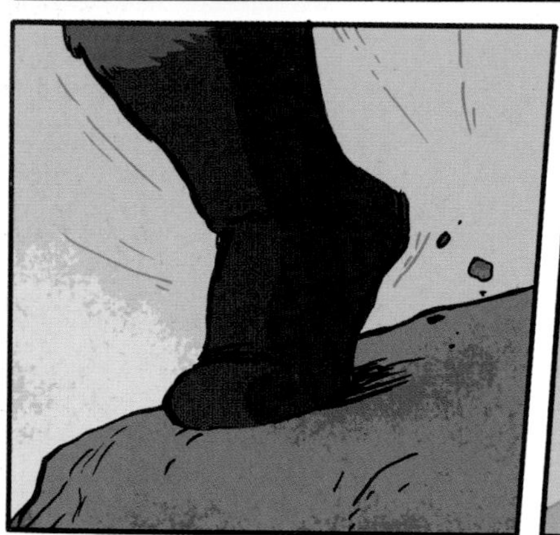

NO TURNING BACK NOW!

RUN!

BRUFF!

ZORA?

NERVOUS?
THE PLAN IS DONE. TRAPS SET. I'M TRYING NOT TO THINK ABOUT IT.
OTHERWISE I MIGHT THROW UP.

I JUST WANTED TO SAY SOMETHING BEFORE I GO.
WE MADE A MISTAKE WITH ULITH. WE WERE UNFAIR. WE ONLY SAW HER AS AN OUTSIDER.

EVEN NOW, IT'S HARD FOR ME TO SEE YOU AS ANYTHING BUT DIFFERENT. BUT YOU'VE DONE SO MUCH FOR PEOPLE YOU HARDLY KNOW.
ALL I ASK IS— IN THE END, DON'T LET BROXO FORGET WHO HE IS.

SEE ANYTHING?
NO.

I... APPRECIATE YOU BEING HERE.

YOUR PLAN IS CRAZY AS IT IS. WITHOUT ME, IT'D BE SUICIDE.

THANKS-

NERVOUS?
SILENCE, BRAT.

LOOK!
WATCH OUT!
SKIIIID!
WELL?!

OH, YES!
YOU WANTED BAD TROUBLE, YOU GOT IT!

CUT THOSE SLINGS WHEN THEY HIT THE GRASS LINE.

WE CAN'T LET THEM INTO THE GORGE TOO EARLY.

IF THAT HAPPENS, WE'RE SUNK.

GET READY!
GRRR

SNARL

MY FATHER SAYS THAT BATTLES ARE ALWAYS SHORTER THAN THEY FEEL.

LET'S FIND OUT!

NOW!

WHOOSH!
TWUNG!
THOR
CRUNCH
UH-OH!

TWUNG!
THOK
CHOOM
KRAK!
SSSSSSSS...

FOR EVERY ONE I HIT, FIVE MORE SEEM TO SPRING UP!

ULITH!

KRAK!
CHOOM!

BROXO'S OKAY!
BE MORE CAREFUL!

GRRRR

ROAR!

TWUNG!
PANG!
SO-
WHOOOO
CHOP!

THE GORGE!
NO!

CHEW!
CHEW!
CHEW!

SNAP!

FOOM!

ZORA, LOOK AROUND! THEY'RE FLOODING INTO THE GORGE, MIGO IS EXHAUSTED, AND I DON'T KNOW HOW MUCH MORE LIGHTNING MY BODY CAN TAKE!

RRRUUUMMBLE

RRRUUUUMMMMBLE
THUNDER?
THERE!
SHLUCK!
RUMBLE!

BROXO!
BOF!
TAKE THIS HORSE TO THE VILLAGE. WE'LL CLEAN UP HERE.

BUT-!
NO TIME!

WE'LL BE OKAY!

SO GET GOING, DUMMY.
DON'T LOOK BACK.

I'M NOT LOSING ANYONE AGAIN.

SOUND THE HORN AND MEET US AT THE LAKE!

CHAPTER 10

THE ANCESTORS ARE DOWN FOR NOW. I'LL HERD THE OLSHEC TO SAFETY. THE REST OF YOU GET GOING.

JOIN US WHEN YOU CAN.

TUT TUT.

IF I WERE LIKE THE ANCESTORS, MY FAMILY WOULD HELP ME.

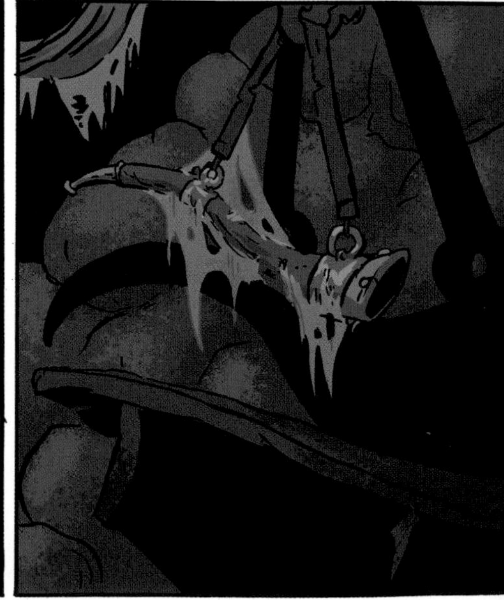

TAROOOOOOOOOO...

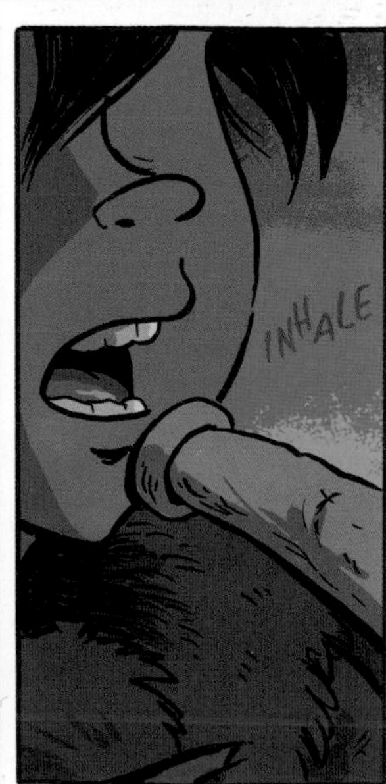
INHALE

WHAM!

CRACK!

UH, ULITH? THANK... THANK YOU. WE ALL MADE IT BECAUSE OF YOUR POWER.

MY POWER? HA... IT´S JUST A MATTER OF TIME, NOW.
WHAT IS?

NOTHING! SILENCE! I´M FINE. I´M FINE!
I´M FINE...

IT´S ALL RIGHT, MASTER.
BREATHE!

THERE IS NO WAY OUT!

HOW CAN I FREE MYSELF?

NO! NO MORE!

WHAT'S GOING ON?
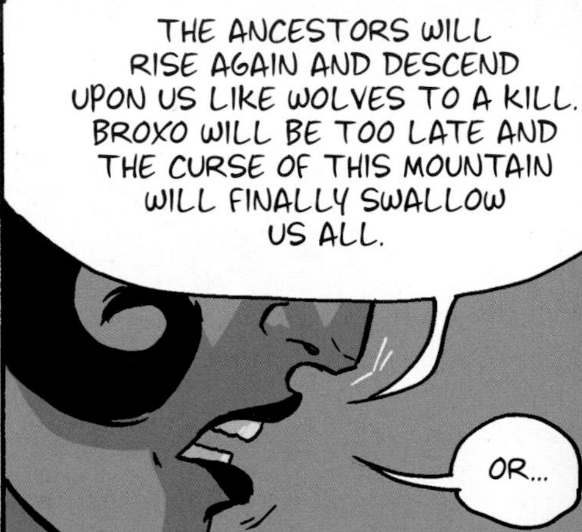
THE ANCESTORS WILL RISE AGAIN AND DESCEND UPON US LIKE WOLVES TO A KILL. BROXO WILL BE TOO LATE AND THE CURSE OF THIS MOUNTAIN WILL FINALLY SWALLOW US ALL.
OR...

WE WILL ESCAPE AND YOU WILL TELL THE PENTHOS THAT I KILLED THE PERYTONS!

YOU'RE CRAZY!
SNARL!

ARROX SAID MY POWERS WERE A GIFT THAT COULD HELP THE CLAN. MAYBE THE WHOLE PENTHOS!

WHY SHOULD I HELP THOSE WHO NEVER HELPED ME?
ULITH, PLEASE...

I KNOW IT WAS UNFAIR THE WAY YOU WERE TREATED. BUT THINGS CAN CHANGE! IT'S NEVER TOO LATE!

THE PERYTON CLAN NEEDS YOU. I NEED YOU.

DO NOT SPEAK LIKE THAT! "NEED"...
WHAT DO YOU *NEED*? RAIN? AM I A TOOL, NOW? LIKE AN AXE OR A SHOVEL?

plip
OR DO YOU NEED SOMETHING ELSE?

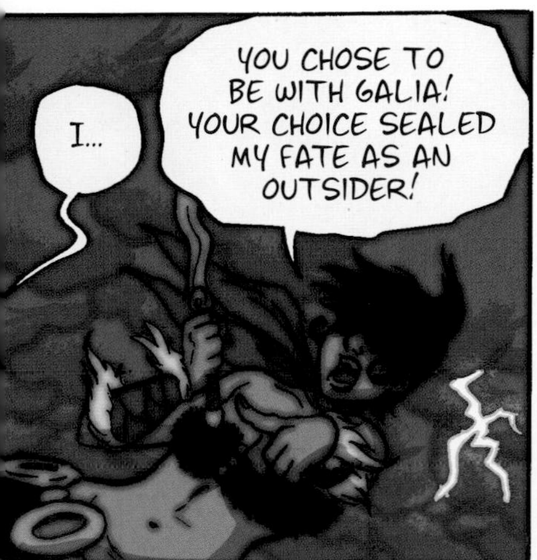
I...
YOU CHOSE TO BE WITH GALIA! YOUR CHOICE SEALED MY FATE AS AN OUTSIDER!

STOP! IT'S NOT LIKE -
I'M NO PERYTON, AND EVEN YOU HAVE FORSAKEN ME! THE STAG WILL NOT COME FOR MY SPIRIT. I WILL ONLY FADE!

THEY CAN KNOW YOU AS I KNOW YOU! I WANT MY NEW SON TO KNOW-

KRA-
KOOM!!

HE LEARNED TOO LATE.

THE STORM
WAS OUT OF MY
CONTROL.

I'D HOPED
IT WOULD KILL
ME, TOO.

BUT WHEN I
AWOKE...

I REALIZED I WASN'T THE ONLY ONE TO DO SO!

THAT'S WHY GLOTH SAID YOU CREATED THE ANCESTORS!
THE CLAN WAS DESTROYED BECAUSE OF MY POWER.

DON'T YOU SEE? I WAS BORN TO CREATE ONLY DEATH!

BOOM

ULITH! TRY TO BE CALM!
LOOK!

THE PERYTONS ARE ALREADY HERE!

BROXO FAILED! NOW WE'LL ALL DIE TOGETHER!
NO...

AAH!

SKREE!

MAGGOT...!

THUNK!

PANT
PANT

RUM MBLE

THERE IS STILL A CHOICE! WHICH DEATH DO YOU CHOOSE, PRINCESS?
THERE *IS* STILL A CHOICE, AND I DON'T CHOOSE ANY DEATH!

WHAT HAPPENED WAS AN ACCIDENT!
A BAD CHOICE! BUT DON'T MAKE ANY MORE!

DON'T LECTURE ME! YOU KNOW NOTHING!

THERE'S STILL A CHANCE TO FIND BROXO AND ESCAPE THE PEAK!
AND WHAT THEN?!

THE OTHER CLANS WILL NEVER ACCEPT ONE THAT IS NOT THEIR OWN! I AM LIVING PROOF!
THE PERYTONS ONLY GOT WHAT I WISHED FOR THEM!

MIGO!
NO!

BOOOM!

NOoo!

MIGO!
OH, MIGO!

WE'RE
ALL DEAD!

WE ALL
MUST DIE!
CHOOM!

HE'S STILL
ALIVE! JUST BE
CALM!

TREMBLE
I... CAN'T!
TOO... MUCH...!

YOU CAN! SEE?
I WON'T ABANDON YOU.
WE'LL GET OUT
OF THIS!

YES...

NICE AND CAL-

AUGH!

BITE!

BOOM!

ZORA!

ZORA!!!

I TRUSTED YOU!

ARROX...?

NO, YOU'RE DEAD!
SPLSH

YOU'RE DEAD!
DODGE!
JAB!

YOU'RE —

KAFF!
SPLASH

ZORA! WAKE UP!

PLEASE!
PLEASE!
PLEASE!

PLEASE! SOMEONE HELP!

DON'T GO!

SHE'S NOT READY TO GO!

WE ONLY EVER LOVED YOU.

COUGH!

HEY...

CHAPTER 11

HA
HA HA!

CRASH
OW!

NOT SO ROUGH! I'M STILL SORE...!

MRR

TAKE CARE OF THE PEAK FOR ME.
I'LL MISS YOU.

YOU DID GOOD, BOY.

OUR PEOPLE CAN REST WHERE THEY BELONG.
WHAT ABOUT YOU?
I, TOO, WILL GO WHERE I BELONG.

BUT WHAT ABOUT ME?
YOUR HEART KNOWS WHERE YOU BELONG. NEVER DESPAIR ABOUT THAT.

TRY NOT TO WISH FOR THE DEAD.

INSTEAD, LOVE THE LIVING.
READY?

WHY CAN'T I RIDE IN FRONT?
BECAUSE YOU DON'T KNOW *HOW*, YET!

KEEP YOUR LEGS TIGHT. HE WON'T APPRECIATE YOU KICKING HIS RIBS THE WHOLE TIME.

HE ALSO NEEDS A NAME. I WAS THINKING WINDRUNNER OR STARJUMPER!
BLEAH!

THOSE ARE GIRLY NAMES!
IS THAT SO?
YES.

I WANT TO NAME HIM *TUHOME*. BECAUSE THAT'S WHERE HE CAN TAKE US.
THAT IS SURPRISINGLY WELL THOUGHT-OUT, FOR YOU.

GRR...
SQUEEZE

WHAT WAS THAT FOR?
NOTHING!

Heaps and mounds of thanks to Calista Brill, Bernadette Baker-Baughman, and Colleen AF Venable for helping turn dough into bread. For Mia Bernardo, Sarah Sapang, Shelli Paroline, Carolyn Moseley, Lynn Lau, and Kenneth Henry, thank you for your help in tanning the hide of this book. To Dave Roman, Bannister and Flo, Scott Price, and the Pelissier Clan, I thank you for your advice, help, and support. And extra special thanks to Mom.

Zack Giallongo was born and raised in Massachusetts, although one half of his family lives in Indiana. Between New England and the Midwest, he's a little bit country, a little bit rock and roll. He currently lives with two cats and enjoys playing the banjo. He also likes cheese, bowling, and writing in the third person. *Broxo* is his first graphic novel.